JEANNE-MARIE GOES TO MARKET

A Story of the West Indies

By

S A R I

GROSSET & DUNLAP

Publishers   NEW YORK

THE sun shown down on the street where Jeanne-Marie was playing. It was a hot sun, for Jeanne-Marie lived in the West Indies. For a time Jeanne-Marie did not notice how hot it was. Then the street began to feel too warm to her bare feet, and the sunlight on the houses hurt her eyes. Jeanne-Marie went into the yard of her own house.

It was shady in the yard and Jeanne-Marie sat down under the mango tree. Looking up through the branches she could see a ripe, yellow mango. How good it would taste! Yes, she could just reach it if she climbed up as high as that low branch. Up she went,

and down she came with the mango in her hand. She sat down under the tree again and bit into the ripe fruit. It was very juicy and soon, all around Jeanne-Marie's mouth was a yellow stain.

A small brown monkey swung from the tree and chattered at Jeanne-Marie.

"So, there you are Tini!" she said. "You want a mango? You shall have a banana instead."

Jeanne-Marie went into the house and came out with a big red banana. The monkey watched her with his bright eyes, then swung himself down from the tree.

"Here, come here, Tini." Jeanne-Marie squatted on the ground and held out the banana. Tini reached for it, held it in his small brown paws and began peeling back the skin.

Jeanne-Marie laughed as he bit into it.

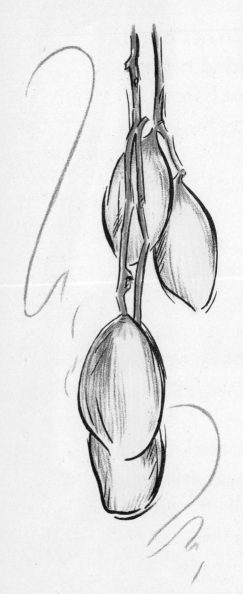

A tall, slim, brown woman came out of the house. On her head was a large water jar. As she walked her body swung easily from side to side, and the jar balanced on her head without even the touch of a hand to steady it. Jeanne-Marie looked up. How beautiful her mother was! And how Jeanne-Marie wished she could balance a water jar on her head! She could carry a basket, but a jar was not so easy.

"Jeanne - Marie," said her mother, "I am going to fetch water. Take care of Pierre, and do not let him crawl in the long grass."

All the time that her mother

was away Jeanne-Marie balanced things on her head. She walked carefully across the yard with a small basket. That was so much easier than the jar. A basket would not break if it fell, but a water jar would break into a thousand pieces. Up and down walked Jeanne-Marie. Pierre watched her. Tini swung himself up into a tree and watched her, too.

The next day was market day. Jeanne-Marie watched her mother as she got ready the big flat basket of fowls to take to the market. The fowls squawked a little, they did not seem to like being packed in the basket with their heads hanging over the edge.

"Let me go to market with you," said Jeanne-Marie. "I can take a basket of mangoes."

"You will drop them," said her mother.

"No, I won't," said Jeanne-Marie. "I can carry a basket very well now."

So she filled her basket with ripe, yellow mangoes and they started for the market.

Along the road they went. Mother's wide bright skirt swung from side to side as she walked. Jeanne-Marie wished she had a wide skirt to swing.

Other women and children came along the road on their way to market. Most of them carried trays and baskets on their heads. Some were leading small grey donkeys.

On each side of the donkeys were baskets, and in the baskets were fruit and vegetables.

Jeanne - Marie was so happy that she forgot all about the basket on her head. She gave a little hop, skip, and jump. Down went the basket and all over the road went the ripe yellow mangoes.

"See what you have done!" said Mother.

Jeanne-Marie stood looking at the mangoes. Then she burst into tears.

"They are all spoiled," she sobbed. "The stones have cut my nice mangoes all to bits."

"Some of them are not cut," said her mother. "Pick up the good ones, Jeanne-Marie."

So Jeanne-Marie picked up the best of the mangoes, put them in her basket and started off again.

This time she walked very carefully, thinking about the basket every minute of the time. Her friend Henri went by, riding

his mother's donkey. He was on his way to market, too.

"Hi!" he called. "Hi! Jeanne-Marie!"

But Jeanne-Marie walked carefully, looking neither to the right nor to the left.

At last they reached the market and Jeanne-Marie was glad to put her basket on the ground.

She looked around her. There was so much to see. So many piles of fruits and vegetables, so many fowls! So many women in wide bright skirts like her mother's! Their tongues kept up a steady chatter as they arranged the things they had brought to sell at the market.

By noon Mother had sold all her fowls. But the mangoes were still in Jeanne-Marie's basket. Jeanne-Marie looked sad.

"Perhaps no one will buy my mangoes," she said.

Just then a stout, smiling woman came along. She was a cook for a white family and she had come to the market to buy food for the day. She stopped by Jeanne-Marie and looked down at her pile of mangoes.

"Good mangoes, honey?" she asked.

"Very good mangoes," said Jeanne-Marie.

Almost before she knew it Jeanne-Marie had sold all her mangoes.

"Now we can go home," said Mother.

It was much easier going home, for everyone had empty baskets. The donkeys trotted along faster with no weight to carry. But it was a long walk and Jeanne-Marie began to be tired. One of the women let her ride on her donkey.

Pretty soon they caught up with Henri on his donkey.

"Hi, Henri!" sang out Jeanne-Marie. "I sold all my mangoes."

"And I sold all my corn!" shouted Henri.

"I like to go to market," said Jeanne-Marie. "Every week my mother will let me go."

"That is if you are careful," said her mother, "and do not drop your basket on the road as you did today."

When they got home Mother went into the house to feed the baby. Jeanne-Marie stayed in the yard and talked to Tini. She told him all about the market.

"I can carry a basket, but what I want to carry is a water jar. Do you think I could ever do that, Tini?"

Jeanne-Marie got one of the water jars that was standing by the steps. She balanced it on her head. She started across

the yard, holding the jar with one hand. Yes, she really could carry it a little way.

So every day Jeanne-Marie carried the jar, and every day she carried it a little better. Every day she watched her mother go to the well and hoped that some day she might go with her.

At last one day Jeanne-Marie could carry the jar all the way across the yard.

"See Tini! I can really carry it." Tini swung from the tree and chattered as if he were trying to say, "I am glad, I am glad, I am glad!"

And, holding the jar very carefully with one hand, Jeanne-Marie followed her mother to the well.